BUILD·A·BEAR
WORKSHOP®
WHERE BEST FRIENDS ARE MADE®

CELE·BEAR·ATE!

Hylas Publishing
129 Main Street
Irvington, New York 10533
www.hylaspublishing.com

Hylas Publishing
Editorial Director: Lori Baird
Art Directors: Edwin Kuo, Gus Yoo
Production Coordinator: Sarah Reilly

Project Credits
Editor: Sarah Reilly
Managing Editor: Myrsini Stephanides
Designer: Shani Parsons

ISBN: 1-59258-135-8

Library of Congress Cataloging-in-Publication Data
available upon request.

Printed and bound in Italy
Distributed by National Book Network

First American Edition published in 2005

10   9   8   7   6   5   4   3   2   1

CELE·BEAR·ATE!

HYLAS

Bears always have a reason to cele·bear·ate

DANCiNG
iS ALWAYS FUN,
EVEN iF YOU
HAVE TWO LEFT
PAWS

7

LOVE IS A
CELE·BEAR·ATION
OF THE
HEART

HAVE A FLAIR FUR THE DRAMATIC

BEARS WILL BE BEARS

A Bear's Smile is Contagious

PRINCESS

15

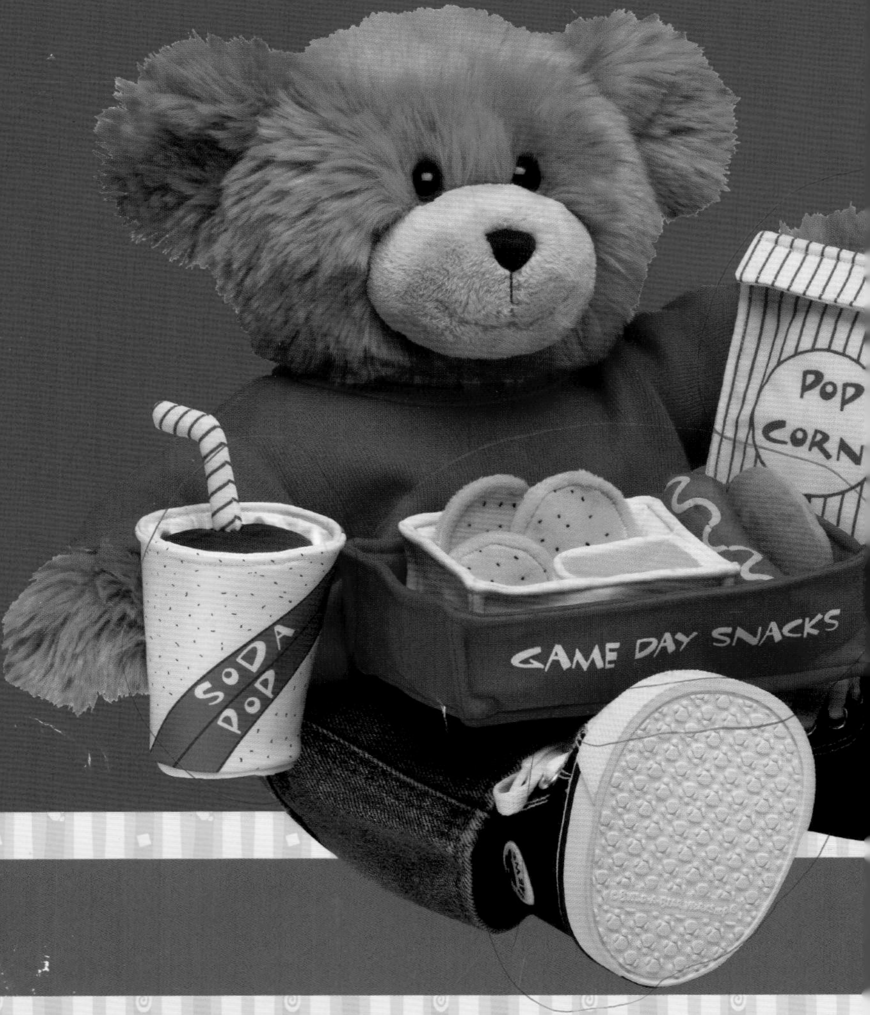
POP CORN
SODA POP
GAME DAY SNACKS

EAT, DRINK AND BE BEARY

ENJOY
EACH DAY
WiTH
FRIENDS

RAISE YOUR PAWS IN THE AIR

RAIN OR SHINE, BEARS ARE ALWAYS READY FOR HUGS

THE WORLD IS A STAGE AND EVERY BEAR PLAYS ITS PART

GOOD STUFF
IS SO MUCH
SWEETER WHEN
CELE·BEAR·ATED
WITH A BEAR

28

iT'S BEARY MERRY WHEN FRIENDS MEET

LEAP INTO
FURRY FUN
EVERY DAY

OTHER BOOKS FROM HYLAS PUBLISHING IN
THE BUILD·A·BEAR WORKSHOP® SERIES:

STUFFED WITH LOVE

FRIENDS FUR LIFE

PAWSITIVE THOUGHTS

BUILD·A·BEAR WORKSHOP®
FURRY FRIENDS HALL OF FAME
THE OFFICIAL COLLECTOR'S GUIDE

Hylas Publishing would like to thank Ginger Bandoni,
Melissa Segal, Lori Zelkind, and Patty Sullivan at
Evergreen Concepts. Many thanks to Laura Kurzu, Mindy
Barsky, and of course, C.E.B. Maxine Clark.